LITTLE GOLDEN BOOK® CLASSICS
Featuring the art of
Feodor Rojankovsky

Three Best-Loved Tales

THE THREE BEARS
A Traditional Nursery Tale

THE COW WENT OVER THE MOUNTAIN
By Jeanette Krinsley

HOP, LITTLE KANGAROO!
By Patricia Scarry

A GOLDEN BOOK • NEW YORK
Western Publishing Company, Inc., Racine, Wisconsin 53404

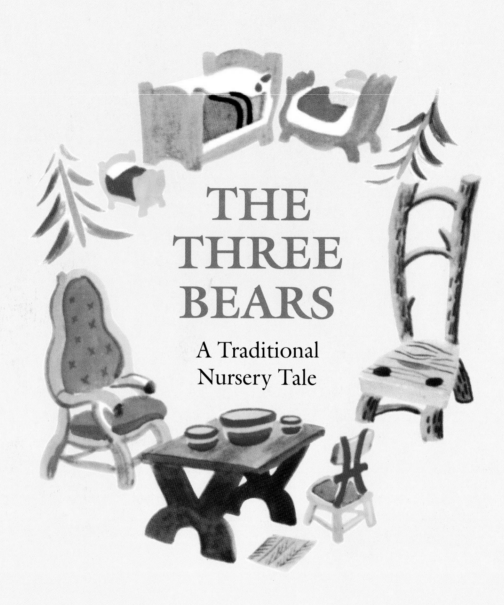

THE THREE BEARS

A Traditional
Nursery Tale

Once upon a time there were three bears—
a great big papa bear, a middle-sized mama bear,
and a wee little baby bear.

They lived in a little house in the forest.

And they had three chairs—a great big chair for the papa bear, a middle-sized chair for the mama bear, and a wee little chair for the baby bear.

And upstairs there were three beds—a great big bed for the papa bear, a middle-sized bed for the mama bear, and a wee little bed for the baby bear.

One morning the mama bear made some
porridge for breakfast.

She filled a great big bowl for the papa bear, a middle-sized bowl for the mama bear, and a wee little bowl for the baby bear.

But the porridge was too hot to eat, so the three bears went out for a walk in the forest.

That same morning a little girl called
Goldilocks was walking through the woods.

She came to the three bears' house. And she
knocked on the door, but nobody called, "Come
in." So she opened the door and went in.

Goldilocks saw the three chairs. She sat in the great big chair. It was too hard. The middle-sized chair was too soft. The baby chair was just right—but it broke when she sat on it.

Now Goldilocks spied the porridge.
"I am hungry," she said.
So she tasted the porridge.
The porridge in the big bowl was too hot.

The porridge in the middle-sized bowl was too cold. The porridge in the wee little bowl was just right—so she ate it all up.

Then Goldilocks went upstairs and tried the beds.

The great big bed was too hard.
The middle-sized bed was too soft.

But the wee little bed was oh, so nice! So
Goldilocks lay down and went to sleep.

Then home through the forest and back to their house came the three bears—the great big bear, the middle-sized bear, and the wee little baby bear.

The moment they stepped into the house,
they saw that someone had been there.

"Humph!" said the papa bear in his great big
voice. "Someone has been sitting in my chair!"

"Land sakes!" said the mama bear in her middle-sized voice. "Someone has been sitting in *my* chair."

"Oh, dear!" cried the baby bear in his wee little voice. "Someone has been sitting in *my* chair, and has broken it all to bits."

Then they all looked at the table.

"Humph," said the papa bear in his great

big voice. "Someone has been tasting my porridge."

"And someone has been tasting *my* porridge," said the mama bear.

"Someone has eaten *my* porridge all up," said
the baby bear sadly.

Then up the stairs went the three bears, with

a thump thump thump,
and a trot trot trot, and a skippity-skip-skip.
(That was the wee little tiny bear.)

"Humph," said the papa bear in his great big voice. "Someone has been sleeping in my bed!"

"And someone has been sleeping in *my* bed," said the mama bear.

"Oh, dear!" cried the baby bear in his wee little voice. "And someone has been sleeping in *my* bed, and here she is right now!"

Goldilocks opened her eyes and she saw the
three bears.

"Oh!" said Goldilocks.

She was so surprised that she jumped right
out of the window and she ran all the way home.
And she never saw the house in the forest again.

THE COW
WENT OVER
THE MOUNTAIN

By Jeanette Krinsley

One day Little Cow said to her mother, "I'm going over to the other mountain. The grass is munchier over there."

"Very well," said Mother Cow.

So away went Little Cow, and soon she met a little frog.

"Come along with me, Little Frog," she said.
"I'm going over to the other mountain. The
bugs are much crunchier there."

So Little Frog jumped up on Cow's back, and they walked along together. Soon they met a little white duck.

"Come with us," said Cow to Little White
Duck. "We are going to the other mountain.
The water is much sploshier there."
So Duck went, too.

Down the road they walked till they met a pig.
"Come along with us, Little Pig," said Cow.
"We are going over to the other mountain. The
mud is much sloshier there."

So Pig went, too, and they walked along
together and sang a silly song.
   "The grass is munchier.
   The bugs are crunchier.

"The water is sploshier.
The mud is sloshier."
Then they saw a bear, so they sang,
"The honey is gooier."

And Bear said, "I'll come, too."
And they walked and walked and walked.

When they got to the other mountain,
they all sat down to rest.

And they were so tired that they soon fell asleep.

In the morning they woke with the sun, very hungry and all ready to eat. BUT—

The grass was not munchier.

The bugs were not crunchier.

The water was not sploshier.

The mud was not sloshier.

The honey was not gooier.

It was just not true, all that Little Cow had said. And everyone felt sad and blue, till all at once Cow jumped up.

"Look," she said. "We are on the wrong mountain." And as she pointed they all agreed that the other mountain was greener.

So they started out again and walked
and walked and walked.

Down, down, down they went till they came
to the bottom of the mountain. Then—

Up, up, up they climbed. Then they stopped,
and what do you think they found?

They were home, on their own green mountain.
So they all looked at Cow and sang—

"The grass is munchier.
The bugs are crunchier.
The water is sploshier.
The mud is sloshier.
The honey is gooier,
Right here at home."

And they laughed and laughed and laughed.

HOP,
LITTLE KANGAROO!

By Patricia Scarry

Bump. Bump. Bump.
Little Kangaroo loved to ride in his mother's front pocket.

It was great fun to sit in that snug, cozy place while his mother hopped about the grassy Australian plains.

One day Mother Kangaroo sat him gently on
the grass and said, "Little One, it is time you
learned to hop. I am going home to make a
sweet berry pie, and I want you to hop home
for supper."

"But I cannot hop," wailed Little Kangaroo.

"Of course you can. You can do anything, if
you try," called Mother.

And away she went, over the hill.

"Ooooh!" howled Little Kangaroo.

But he did not try to hop. He sat very still and he felt very cross.

Soon a fat little Dingo pup waddled up the hill.

"Please, will you carry me home?" asked Little
Kangaroo.

"Carry you!" grinned the Dingo. "No sirree!"

"But I have not learned to hop," sighed Little
Kangaroo.

"You must try. Follow me," called the Dingo.
"Hop, Little Kangaroo!"

But Little Kangaroo did not try to hop.
A friendly Koala Bear called down from her tree, "If you cannot hop, Little Kangaroo, perhaps you could swing from tree to tree."

And she very nicely lowered a vine to Little Kangaroo.

"Now hold tight and swing!" called Koala Bear.

"Be careful!" cried the Cockatoo from a nearby branch.

"Wheeee!"

Little Kangaroo sailed through the air.

He reached for the next tree and missed it.

BUMP!

"Poor Little Kangaroo," said the gentle
Cuscus. "What are you trying to do?"

"I want to go home for my supper," cried
Little Kangaroo, "but I cannot hop."

"Perhaps you can fly home, like me," shrilled the Cockatoo.

"It's easy to fly. Just spread your arms wide and lean into the wind, like this."

Up, up, up went the Cockatoo.

Down, down, down, SPLASH! into the pond, fell Little Kangaroo.

It was lucky for Little Kangaroo that a large Jabiru had seen him fall.

She scooped him from the water with her strong beak and dropped him on the bank to dry.

"Boo-hoo!" cried Little Kangaroo. "I am wet and hungry and I want to go home."

"Poor Little Kangaroo," whispered the Sugar Glider, peeping from her hollow.

"Hahahahaha!" tittered the Laughing
Kookaburra.

"Hush, you foolish bird," said the Possum.
"You must not laugh at a Little Kangaroo who
cannot hop, or fly like a bird, or swim like a fish,
or climb in the trees, like me."

"I will help you get home, Little Kangaroo,"
said a furry Wombat. "If you cannot hop over the
hill, I will dig a tunnel through the hill for you."

And the helpful little Wombat went to work, digging a hole in the hill.

How the earth flew!

"Soon I will be home, eating Mother's berry pie," thought Little Kangaroo happily.

Then Little Kangaroo put himself inside the hole. He wiggled, and he waggled.

"Oh, dear, he is stuck," wailed the Bandicoot.

It was true. Little Kangaroo could not tunnel home. His sad tail wagged helplessly.

Tug! Tug! Tug!
His friends pulled on his long, hurting tail.

And out of that big black hole in the hill popped Little Kangaroo.

"Oh, how will I ever get home?" he groaned.

"You must hop, like this," said the Bunny. "Hop, Little Kangaroo!"

Just then, Mother Kangaroo appeared at the top of the hill.

She stood there and called, "Hoo hoo! Look what I made for you, Little One."

Oh, Little Kangaroo was so happy to see his mommy!

He could not wait to eat that sweet berry pie.

"Why, Little One, you are hopping," smiled Mother.

And Little Kangaroo was so surprised that he tumbled and fell.

But he got right up again and hopped all the way to his mother, and that delicious berry pie.

"You can do anything, if you try," said Mother.
And proudly they hopped away home.

About Feodor Rojankovsky

T wo great events determined the course of my childhood," Feodor
Rojankovsky once said. "I was taken to the zoo and saw the most
marvelous creatures on earth: bears, tigers, monkeys, and reindeer; and, while
my admiration was running high, I was given a set of color crayons."

Rojankovsky, who went on to become one of the most popular children's
book illustrators in America, was born in Mitava, Latvia, in 1891. As a child, he
developed both a love of drawing and a passionate interest in nature.

Rojankovsky enrolled at the Moscow Academy of Fine Art in 1914, but his
studies were soon interrupted by World War I. Forced to leave Russia after the
war, he worked as a stage designer in Poland and then as an art director and
illustrator for several publishing houses in France.

In 1941, after the German occupation of Paris, Rojankovsky emigrated to
the United States, where he was associated with the Artists and Writers Guild
and illustrated some of the first Little Golden Books. Along with keen
observations of nature, his work reveals a strong Russian folk art influence.
That influence is especially clear in his version of *The Three Bears,* included in
this volume.

By the time he died in 1970, Rojankovsky had illustrated well over one
hundred children's books, including nearly two dozen handsome titles for
Golden Books. His interpretation of *Frog Went A-Courtin',* published by
Harcourt, Brace and Company in 1956, won him the Caldecott Medal, the
most prestigious award given to a children's book illustrator.